HANSEL AND GRETEL

THE BROTHERS GRIMM

Illustrated by Anthony Browne

ALFRED A. KNOPF ❧ NEW YORK

THIS IS A BORZOI BOOK PUBLISHED BY ALFRED A. KNOPF, INC.

Copyright © 1981 by Anthony Browne. All rights reserved under International and Pan-American Copyright Conventions. Published in the United States by Alfred A. Knopf, Inc., New York, and simultaneously in Canada by Random House of Canada Limited, Toronto. Distributed by Random House, Inc., New York. Originally published in Great Britain by Julia MacRae Books, London, in 1981. Adapted from the translation by Eleanor Quarrie; first published by the Folio Society in 1949. Library of Congress Cataloging-in-Publication Data.   Hänsel und Gretel. English. Hansel and Gretel. Translation of: Hänsel und Gretel. "Adapted from the translation by Eleanor Quarrie." Summary: A poor woodcutter's two children, lost in the woods, come upon a gingerbread house inhabited by a wicked witch. With illustrations showing characters with modern dress and possessions. [1. Fairy tales. 2. Folklore—Germany] I. Grimm, Jacob, 1785–1863. II. Grimm, Wilhelm, 1786–1859. III. Browne, Anthony, ill. IV. Title. PZ8.H196 1988 [398.2] [E] 87-25993 ISBN 0-394-89859-1 ISBN 0-394-99859-6 (lib. bdg.) Manufactured in the United States of America 10 9 8 7 6 5 4 3 2 1

AT THE EDGE of a large forest lived a poor woodcutter with his two children and their stepmother. The boy's name was Hansel, and the girl's name was Gretel.

The family was always very poor, and when a terrible famine came to the land, they could find nothing to eat.

The woodcutter lay fretting in bed at night, tossing and turning. He sighed and said to his wife: "What's going to happen to us? How can we feed our children when we haven't enough for ourselves?"

"I'll tell you what," said the wife, "early tomorrow morning we'll take the children out into the thickest part of the forest. We'll make them a fire and give them each a little piece of bread. Then we'll go to our work and leave them alone. They will never find their way home, and we'll be rid of them."

"No! I won't do it," he said. "How could I bring myself to leave my children alone in the forest? The wild animals would soon come and eat them."

"You fool!" said the wife. "Then we must all four die of hunger. You may as well cut the planks for our coffins." She gave him no peace until he consented.

"But I'm grieved for the poor children," he said.

Hunger had kept the children awake, too, and they heard what their stepmother said to their father. Gretel cried bitterly and said to Hansel, "It's all over for us now."

"Quiet, Gretel," whispered Hansel. "Don't be upset. I'll find a way to save us."

After their parents had gone to sleep, Hansel got up, put on his robe, and crept out the front door. The moon was shining brightly and the white pebbles around the house glittered like new coins. Hansel stooped and filled his pockets with as many as they would hold. Then he went back to bed, saying to Gretel, "It's all right now, little sister. Go back to sleep. God will help us."

At daybreak, before the sun had risen, the woman came and wakened the children. "Get up, you lazybones, we must go to the forest to fetch wood." She gave them each a small piece of bread, saying, "Here's something for you to eat, but don't have it too soon, for you'll get nothing else." Gretel put the bread inside her coat, and Hansel put all the pebbles into his trouser pockets. Then they set out together for the forest.

When they had gone a little way, Hansel stood still and looked back at the house. He did this again and again.

"Hansel, why are you lagging behind?" asked his father. "Watch what you're doing and keep up with us."

"I'm looking at my white cat," said Hansel. "It's on the roof, saying good-bye to me."

"You idiot!" said the wife. "That's not the cat. It's the morning sun shining on the chimney." But Hansel was not really looking at a cat, for each time he stopped he had dropped a white pebble onto the path.

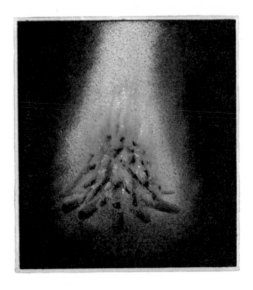

When they were deep in the forest, their father said, "Hansel and Gretel, you go and collect some wood and I'll make a fire to keep you warm." The children gathered some brushwood into a great pile, and when it was blazing the woman said, "Now lie down by the fire, children, and have a good rest. We're going farther into the forest to chop wood. When we've finished, we'll come back and fetch you."

Hansel and Gretel sat by the fire, and at midday they both ate their bread. Because they could hear the blows of an axe, they thought that their father was nearby. But it was not an axe. It was a branch that he had fastened to a withered tree so that the wind blew it to and fro. After Hansel and Gretel had been sitting for a long time, their eyes closed with weariness, and they fell asleep. When they awoke it was very dark. Gretel began to cry, saying, "How shall we ever get out of the woods?"

Hansel comforted her. "Wait a little, till the moon is up, then we'll soon find the way."

Once the full moon had risen, Hansel took his little sister by the hand and followed the pebbles, which shone in the moonlight and showed them the way.

The children walked all through the night and at daybreak reached home. They knocked at the door, and when the stepmother looked out and saw who it was, she said, "You wicked children! Why did you sleep so long in the forest? We thought you were never coming home."

But their father was glad, for it had broken his heart to leave them behind all alone.

Not long afterward there was widespread famine again, and the children heard their stepmother talking to their father in bed at night. "We have only half a loaf left. After that there is nothing. The children must go. We'll take them deeper into the forest this time so that they can't possibly find their way back. There's nothing else we can do." It grieved the man terribly, for he thought it would be better to share the last crust with his children. But his wife would not listen to anything he said. She scolded and reproached him, and because he had consented the first time, he was forced to agree once more.

The children were still awake and overheard them talking. When the adults had gone to sleep, Hansel got up to collect pebbles as before, but the woman had locked the door and he could not get out. Still he comforted his little sister. "Don't cry, Gretel. God will help us again."

Early in the morning the woman roused the children from bed and gave each of them a piece of bread, smaller than before. On the way to the forest Hansel crumbled his piece in his pocket, often stopping to drop the crumbs on the ground.

"Hansel," said his father, "why do you keep stopping and looking around? Come on!"

"I'm looking at my little dove that is sitting on the roof saying good-bye to me," said Hansel.

"Nonsense!" said the stepmother. "That's not a dove. It's the morning sun shining on the chimney." But Hansel continued to drop the crumbs as he went along.

The children were led deeper into the forest, deeper than they had ever been before. A fire was lit, and the stepmother said, "Stay by the fire. You can sleep for a while if you're tired. We're going farther into the forest to cut some wood, and we'll come back and fetch you later."

At noon Gretel shared her bread with Hansel, who had strewn his along the path. Then they went to sleep. Evening passed, but nobody came for the children. It was dark when they woke up. Hansel again comforted his sister, saying, "Wait till the moon is up, Gretel. Then we'll see the crumbs I scattered, and they'll show us the way home."

When the moon rose they set off, but there were no bread crumbs, for the birds who lived in the forest had eaten them all. "Cheer up," said Hansel, "we'll soon find the way." But they could not.

They walked all through that night and the next day, unable to get out of the forest. They were very hungry but could find only a few berries to eat. The children became so tired that they could go no farther. They lay down under a tree and went to sleep.

It was the third morning since they had left home and still they walked on, deeper and deeper into the forest. If help did not come soon, they would perish. At midday they saw a beautiful snow-white bird perched on a branch, singing so sweetly that they stopped to listen. After a while it flew away and they followed it until they came to a little house, where the bird perched on the roof. When Hansel and Gretel went closer they could see that the house was made of bread, the roof was cake, and the windowpanes were clear sugar.

"Look at that," said Hansel. "A feast! I'll try a piece of the roof; you can eat some of the window." He stretched up and broke off a bit of the roof to see how it tasted. Gretel stood by the window and nibbled it. Then a low voice called from inside the house:

"Nibble, nibble, little mouse,
Who is gnawing at my house?"

The children answered:

"Only the wind,
The heaven-sent wind."

And they went on eating. Hansel pulled down a huge piece of the roof, while Gretel took out a whole windowpane and sat down to enjoy it.

From another window an old woman watched them. Suddenly the door opened and she hobbled out. Hansel and Gretel were so terrified that they dropped the food. But the old woman shook her head and said, "Well, my dear children, who brought you here? Come in and stay with me. No harm will come to you." She took them by the hand and drew them indoors.

A meal of milk, pancakes and sugar, apples and nuts, was spread out on the table. After they had eaten, Hansel and Gretel were shown two pretty little beds, where they lay down and thought themselves in heaven.

The old woman's kindness was only pretense, for she was really a wicked witch who lay in wait for children. She had built the bread house in order to lure them to her, and when a child fell into her power she would kill it, cook it, and eat it, and make a great treat of the day. Witches always know when humans are near, for although they are red-eyed and short-sighted they have a keen sense of smell, like an animal.

The witch was up early in the morning, before the children were awake, and when she saw them sleeping so sweetly, she muttered to herself, "That will make a tasty dish." She seized Hansel with her skinny hand, dragged him outside to a little cage, and locked him in. He screamed and screamed as loud as he could, but it was no use. Then the witch went to Gretel, shook her awake, and shouted, "Get up, lazybones! Fetch some water and cook something nice for your brother. He's outside in the cage and has to be fattened. When he's fat enough I shall eat him." Gretel began to cry, but all in vain; she had to do what the wicked witch told her.

All the best food was now cooked for poor Hansel, while Gretel got nothing but scraps. Every morning the witch would go out to the cage and call out, "Hansel, put out your finger so that I can feel if you are fat enough." But Hansel would hold out a little bone, and the witch, whose eyes were dim, thought it was his finger and was surprised that he did not fatten up.

When four weeks had passed and Hansel was still thin, she lost patience and would wait no longer. "Gretel!" she called. "Be quick and fetch water. Thin or fat, Hansel will be killed and cooked tomorrow."

Tears streamed down Gretel's face as she carried the water. "Dear God, please help us," she cried. "If the wild animals in the forest had eaten us, at least we would have died together."

"Stop your blubbering," said the witch. "There's no help for you."

Early the next morning Gretel had to get up to light the fire and fill the kettle. The witch said, "We will bake first. I have heated the oven and kneaded the dough." She pushed Gretel toward the oven, saying, "Crawl in and see if it's hot enough to put the bread in." She meant to shut the oven door when Gretel was inside, and roast her, and eat her as well. But Gretel saw what the witch had in mind and said, "I don't know how to do it. How do I get in?"

"Stupid girl!" said the witch. "The door is easily big enough. See, I could get in myself." She climbed onto a stool and put her head into the oven. Then Gretel gave her a great push which sent her right in, banged shut the iron door, and locked it.

Gretel ran straight to Hansel, opened his cage, and cried, "Hansel, we're free. The old witch is dead!" He rushed out, like a bird set free, and they hugged and kissed each other with joy.

There was nothing more to be afraid of, so they went into the witch's house. In every corner were chests full of pearls and jewels. "These are better than pebbles," said Hansel as he crammed his pockets full. Gretel also filled her pockets with as much as they could hold, and they hurried away from the house.

After a few hours' journey through the forest, they came to a great stretch of water. "We can't get across," said Hansel. "There's no bridge."

"There doesn't seem to be a boat either," said Gretel. "But look, there's a white duck. If I ask her, she'll help us across." She called out:

> *"Little duck, little duck,*
> *Here stand Hansel and Gretel.*
> *There is no bridge upon our track,*
> *Take us over on your white back."*

The duck swam up. Hansel sat on it and told his sister to join him.

"No, we would be too heavy for the duck," said Gretel. "Let her take us one at a time."

When both of them were across and had gone a little farther on, the forest began to grow more and more familiar to them until at last they saw their father's house in the distance. They began to run. They rushed inside and threw their arms around their father. He had not had a moment of happiness since he had left his children in the forest. The stepmother, however, had died.

Hansel and Gretel took the pearls and jewels from their pockets and scattered them all over the room. Their worries were over, and they lived together in perfect happiness.

My tale is done; see the mouse run;
Catch it if you would, to make a fur hood.